ROSIE WOODS

in Little Red Writing Hood

written by Maya Myers
illustrated by Eleanor Howell

raintree
a Capstone company — publishers for children

In loving memory of my own Mrs Marshall,
who made me believe I could be a really great writer
– MM

Raintree is an imprint of Capstone Global Library Limited, a company incorporated in England and Wales having its registered office at 264 Banbury Road, Oxford, OX2 7DY – Registered company number: 6695582

www.raintree.co.uk
myorders@raintree.co.uk

Designed by Sarah Bennett
Printed and bound in India

978 1 3982 5661 3

British Library Cataloguing in Publication Data
A full catalogue record for this book is available from the British Library.

Contents

FUN FACTS
ABOUT ME, ROSIE WOODS

1. I love to write in my trusty red notebook.
2. I am quiet. My friend Wolfie is ...not.
3. I live with my dad, and I can walk
   to my grandma's house.
4. My teacher, Mrs Marshall, is the GOAT
   (greatest of all time)!
5. The story you are about to read happened
   in our classroom.

Chapter One

The secret ingredient

Rosie Woods liked nothing better than getting lost in a good book. She loved the way a story could make her forget about everything around her. She loved the thrill of her heart beating faster when a story took her on a new adventure in an exciting place with interesting characters.

But Rosie was not a fan of excitement in real life. She was quiet. She liked quiet places and quiet people. So, from time to time, she found her friend Wolfie a little bit . . . challenging.

Wolfie lived down the road. He was really friendly to everybody. Rosie liked playing with Wolfie because he made her laugh. He didn't seem to mind that she was quiet. He did enough talking for both of them.

In fact, Wolfie almost never *stopped* talking. He was the biggest chatterbox in Rosie's class. He talked on the way to school, he talked during class, he talked during breaktime and he talked all the way home.

Once in a while, Wolfie came over to play. After he left, Rosie's dad would shake his head and laugh. "That Wolfie," he'd say. And Rosie would just say, "Yep."

Sometimes, though, all that talking got a little bit much for Rosie. Plus,

Wolfie had this habit of telling Rosie things she already knew.

At school on Monday, Mrs Marshall told the class they would be learning to write stories. At the end of the week, they would each write a story of their own.

This sounded like the perfect assignment for Rosie! She loved stories so much that she was sure she could write a good one.

Mrs Marshall said their stories needed four things. Rosie took notes in her trusty red notebook.

EVERY STORY NEEDS:

SETTING: where the story happens

HERO: most important character

PROBLEM: something wrong that the hero has to fix or solve

SOLUTION: how they fix it

Wolfie sat at the same table as Rosie. He leaned over to peek at her notes.

"The hero is the one who saves the day," he whispered loudly.

Rosie gave a very small nod while she made her eyes super big to tell Wolfie he should hush. But he wasn't very good at body language.

"I could be the hero in a story," Wolfie continued. "I could totally save the day. I'm the best at solving problems. I would always get the bad guy."

Rosie put a finger to her lips and raised her eyebrow towards Mrs Marshall, who had an eyebrow raised towards Wolfie. (Mrs Marshall was excellent at body language.)

But instead of being quiet, Wolfie called out to Mrs Marshall, "Hey, how come there's no bad guy on that list?"

Mrs Marshall silently put her hand in the air and waited for Wolfie to do the same. When he did, she said, "Yes, Wolfie?"

"How come you don't have a bad guy on the list?" he repeated. "You know, like a villain? Every story needs a villain."

Mrs Marshall nodded. "A story *can* have a villain. That would be one kind of problem. But there are other kinds of problems too. What are some other kinds of problems a hero might have to solve?"

While other children in the class were naming problems, such as tornadoes and bad grades and bad breath, Rosie read over her notes again. *Setting, hero, problem, solution.* Those were all important, she knew. But she felt like something was missing.

Wolfie leaned over to Rosie. "Hey, who's your favourite bad guy?"

Rosie gave Wolfie a little scowl.

She was trying to listen to everyone's problem ideas. And who has a favourite bad guy, anyway? *That Wolfie.* If there was anything predictable about him, it was that he was unpredictable.

Unpredictable! That was it, Rosie thought – the thing that made a story really good. She loved it when a story didn't quite go the way she expected. All her favourite stories had a clever twist in them.

Rosie wanted to tell Mrs Marshall about the twist. But when she thought about raising her hand, her tummy made a different kind of twist. She decided to keep her idea to herself. It would be Rosie's secret ingredient.

She added the twist to her list, but she used a code, to keep it secret.

At the end of class, Mrs Marshall said, "Your homework is to brainstorm story ideas! Who can remind us what it means to brainstorm?"

Wolfie's arm waved wildly in the air, but his mouth did not wait to be called on. "Oh, me, me! Brainstorm is like – it's like a storm in your brain! Like, BOOM, thunder, lightning, WHOA! And then all the ideas that are in the storm, you write 'em down."

Wolfie grinned proudly and nodded at Rosie. Rosie smiled and wiggled her eyebrows to show she liked his answer. *That Wolfie*, she thought.

Half of Mrs Marshall's face twitched as she pressed her lips together. "Thank you, Wolfie," she said. "And remember: every idea has potential, so write them *all* down – good or bad."

Why would you write down a bad idea? Rosie wondered.

Rosie turned to a new page and wrote *BRAINSTORM* across the top.

Rosie was excited. She thought she might be able to write one of the best stories in the whole class. She had a secret ingredient.

Now all she needed was a good idea.

Chapter Two

Brainstorm

On the bus journey home, Rosie opened her notebook. She found a sharp pencil and got ready to start brainstorming. She wrote numbers down the side of the page for all the ideas she was going to have.

She tapped her pencil on the tip of her nose. *Here we go*, she thought. *First idea . . .*

"Hey, Rosie!" Wolfie popped up over the seat in front of her. "What's your story going to be about?"

Rosie shrugged. "Don't know yet."

Wolfie looked down at her notes. "Is it about ice cream?"

"Nope." Rosie shook her head and closed her notebook. She didn't want Wolfie to guess her secret ingredient.

"You *could* write a story about ice cream, though," Wolfie said. "It could be about a kid who eats so much ice cream that they turn into an ice-cream cone and their best friend eats them. Wouldn't that be awesome?"

"I guess," Rosie said. It sounded kind of scary to her.

Wolfie sat back down in his seat, and Rosie opened her notebook again. She started to think of a new idea. *Once there was a –*

This time Wolfie's head came round the side of the seat. "Mrs Marshall said we have to brainstorm. That means we think of lots of ideas."

"Uh-huh," Rosie said, closing her notebook again.

"Even if they're good or bad," Wolfie said.

"I know, Wolfie," Rosie said. "I was at school today too, remember?"

"Oh, yeah!" said Wolfie. He laughed and turned back round.

Rosie opened up her notebook. *Number one. How about –*

Wolfie threw his head backwards over the top of his seat, so he was looking at Rosie upside down. "Oh man, I have so many ideas, I don't know which one to write first!"

That Wolfie. He brainstormed out loud the whole way home.

Maybe the villain is this DRAGON that comes and eats all the people in this town and the hero is a knight boy who has to DEFEAT the dragon, OR maybe the villain is this MONSTER that lives under the stairs and the hero is the ordinary boy who lives in the house and he has to FIGHT the monster, OR maybe . . .

Rosie couldn't hear her own ideas over all of Wolfie's. By the time they got to their stop, Rosie's list was still empty.

"Bye, Rosie!" Wolfie said. "Tomorrow, on the way to school, you can tell me all *your* story ideas!"

Rosie waved. She hoped she would have some by then.

Chapter Three

Into the woods

At home, Rosie hung her backpack on the hook and gave her dad a hug.

"Hi, kid. Got homework?" he asked.

Rosie nodded. "I need story ideas," she said.

"Well, you know who can help you with that," Dad said.

"Yep!" said Rosie, raising her eyebrows twice at Dad. Rosie was lucky: not only did her grandma live just over the other side of the park, but she was *also* a librarian. Gram knew all there was to know about stories.

"I'll let her know you're coming." Dad sent Gram a text, pulled Rosie in for a squeeze, then turned back to his work. "Home by dinner, kid," he said.

Last summer, Dad had decided that Rosie was old enough to walk to Gram's all by herself. Rosie liked going alone, especially when she got past the playground, over the creek and onto the walking trail that went through the trees.

When she got to the very middle of the trail, she could hear Gram's wind chimes before she could see Gram's house. She could still hear children shouting from the playground, but she could see only trees around her. Rosie listened to the rustling leaves and breathed in the earthy smells. She imagined she was deep in a forest. She thought about the

animals that might be hiding behind a
bush or down in a hole or up in a tree.
She wondered what she would do if one
of them stepped onto the path, like a
hedgehog or a deer – or even a wolf.

Imagining what might happen in the

forest felt like having a secret adventure. It was kind of like being scared, but in an exciting way. Just enough to make her heart beat a little harder and her feet move a little faster.

Lots of Rosie's favourite stories had a forest in them. And, just then, she decided her story would too.

She leaned her notebook against a tree and wrote down her setting.

EVERY STORY NEEDS:
SETTING: where the story happens FOREST
HERO: most important character
PROBLEM: something wrong that the
            hero has to fix or solve
SOLUTION: how they fix it

Chapter Four

Food for thought

Gram's house was one of the best places in Rosie's world. It was filled with books, and Gram brought new ones home from the library all the time. There was a cosy reading nook under the stairs *and* a hammock to read in outside. Plus, Gram's house always smelled of biscuits. They were usually healthy biscuits – brain food, Gram called them – but healthy biscuits were better than no biscuits at all.

Rosie burst in through the kitchen door.

Gram was sitting at the table with a big pile of books. "Hello, my little red Rose!" Gram said, as she always did.

"Hi, Gram." Rosie gave Gram a hug.

"Good day at school?" Gram asked.

"Pretty good. But I've got work to do," Rosie said. "We're supposed to brainstorm story ideas."

"What fun!" Gram said. "How's it going so far?"

Rosie opened her notebook to show Gram.

Gram eyed the empty list, then looked at Rosie. "You need some brain food." She waved a hand towards the cooling rack on the counter. "Flaxseed-date-carob gems. Still warm."

"Today it's brain*storming* food," Rosie said, giving her eyebrows a double raise.

"That it is," said Gram with a laugh.

Rosie put two of the very heavy biscuits on a plate and went to sit in the reading nook.

She fluffed up her pillows and got comfortable. She took out her coloured pencils and made sure they were all sharp. She ate a biscuit. She coloured in her secret ingredient. She drew some trees to help show her setting. She ate the second biscuit. Her mouth was feeling quite dry. Rosie went back to the kitchen for a glass of oat milk.

"How's that brainstorming coming?" Gram asked.

Rosie blew out a big breath. "It's not."

"Well, why not?"

Rosie hung her head. "I don't know where to start."

"Easy – wherever you are!" said
Gram. "Brainstorming is about starting
anywhere. You write down *all* your
ideas, whether they're good or bad."

Rosie looked sideways at Gram. "That's what Mrs Marshall says. But why would I write down a *bad* idea?"

"You never know," said Gram. "A bad idea *could* turn into a good one."

"But I don't want bad ideas, Gram. I want a *good* idea, so I can write a *good* story."

Gram put her hands up. "I'm sure you know best, my little red Rose."

Rosie narrowed her eyes at Gram. That was what Gram said anytime Rosie started to argue. And as usual, it was the end of the argument.

Gram smiled at Rosie. "Just to get started, how about you look around and write down some of the things you see?"

Rosie thought that sounded stupid, but she wasn't about to say so to Gram.

And she had to put *something* on her list. She looked at the table and wrote the first thing she saw.

> 1. books

Stories are *in* books. She couldn't write a story *about* a book.

> 1. books
> 2. Gram

Gram was a hero to Rosie, but she didn't want to write a story about a grandmother.

> 1. books
> 2. Gram
> 3. biscuits

Rosie remembered what Wolfie had said about ice cream. She imagined eating so many of Gram's biscuits that she turned into a biscuit and Wolfie tried to eat her!

Rosie shuddered. She didn't want to write a scary story.

1. books
2. Gram
3. biscuits
4. oat milk

Where did oat milk even come from? Rosie giggled, imagining teeny-tiny fairy milkmaids squeezing the milk out of each little oat. But she didn't want to write a silly story either.

Ugh. These were bad ideas, alright. Rosie hoped Mrs Marshall wouldn't call on her to share them tomorrow.

Chapter Five

The crumb collector

In class on Tuesday, Rosie listened carefully to everyone's ideas.

Tai wanted to write about a scientist who invents an invisibility potion but then no one can find her because she's invisible.

Reggie wanted to write about a garden that only grows sweets and the monster that guards it.

Nela wanted to write about a skydiving panda that dives into outer space.

Wolfie rattled off four different ideas

before Mrs Marshall put a hand up and told him she was glad he had been thinking about it and that was enough to share.

All the children's ideas were pretty good. Better than anything on Rosie's list, at least. Rosie was relieved that Mrs Marshall didn't call on her.

But when Mrs Marshall asked the class if they remembered the four story parts they had talked about, Rosie raised her hand.

"Yes, Rosie?"

"Setting, hero, problem, solution," Rosie said softly. *And a clever twist,* she thought.

"That's right!" Mrs Marshall's eyes twinkled at Rosie.

Mrs Marshall told them that their

homework for tonight was to decide on those four parts for their own stories.

Rosie already knew her setting. But she didn't have any ideas about heroes, problems or solutions. Or clever twists. She had some work to do.

At Gram's after school, Rosie took her millet-apricot-walnut biscuits out to the hammock and hung upside down to get the blood moving in her brain. Boy, was it hard to eat a dry biscuit upside down! Most of it ended up in her hair.

Rosie turned herself over, cleared her throat and opened her notebook. As she read through her not-so-great ideas, she pulled the strings of her hoodie tighter and tighter, until only one eye could see out. When she scanned that eye over the garden to find something to write

about, she caught a little movement. She
loosened her hood strings so that she
could use both eyes.

A little mouse was poking its head
out from under Gram's porch. Rosie
sat very still – as still as she could sit
in a hammock. The mouse looked left

and right, its tiny black eyes glistening in the sun, then it scurried into the grass. The mouse stopped . . . then came closer . . . and closer, until it was right under Rosie! She peered over the edge of the hammock. The mouse was munching on Rosie's biscuit crumbs!

"Hello, mouse," Rosie whispered. "I bet that's your kind of biscuit!"

The mouse turned its tiny, twitching pink nose up to Rosie. Then it went back to filling its cheeks. When all the crumbs had gone, it scampered back under the porch.

Wow! thought Rosie. She had never been so close to a mouse before. She wondered whether the mouse was going to eat all those crumbs in her cheeks now or save some for later.

She wondered whether the mouse's house was full of crumbs and other goodies. She wondered whether there were babies to feed in the mouse's house. Then she wondered whether there was even a mouse house at all, or just a hole, or a nest . . .

All these questions got her wondering whether she might be able to write a story about a mouse. She added it to her list.

1. books
2. Gram
3. biscuits
4. oat milk
5. mouse eating biscuits

Rosie wasn't sure it was the *best* idea, but she had a feeling it had . . . What had Mrs Marshall said? *Potential.* That was it.

On the opposite page, she made a note.

HERO: most important character   MOUSE?

She used a question mark because she wasn't quite sure.

Rosie ran inside to tell Gram about the mouse.

"You see?" Gram said. "*Everyone* loves my brain food!"

Rosie laughed. "Gram, I was wondering: do you think a mouse could be a hero?"

"For your story, you mean?"

Rosie nodded.

"Well," Gram said, dipping a biscuit into her tea, "what makes a good hero?"

"I don't know," Rosie said. "A hero should be brave, I s'pose? And strong." Her shoulders slumped. "A mouse isn't very strong, though." Maybe it wasn't a good idea after all.

Gram put up a wait-just-a-minute finger. "Don't forget clever," she said. "Sometimes clever is better than strong."

"Hey!" said Rosie. *Just like my clever twist!* she thought.

"What?" Gram asked.

"Oh, nothing." Rosie grinned. "Just my secret ingredient."

Gram chuckled. "Well, you've done it now."

Huh? Rosie thought.

"The first important thing for storytelling," Gram said, reading her mind.

Rosie's nose wrinkled. "What's that?"

Gram's eyes sparkled. "You've got me intrigued."

"What's intrigued?" Rosie asked.

"It means I'm curious to know more," said Gram.

Rosie gave a double brows-up. "Me too!"

Chapter Six

What if?

On the bus on Wednesday morning, Rosie was feeling anxious. She had decided to write her story about a mouse. And she had decided the story would take place in the forest. She had drawn a lot of little pictures of mice. And trees. But she didn't really know what would *happen* to the mouse in the forest. She only had two of the four parts worked out for her story, and Mrs Marshall would be checking their notebooks today.

Wolfie didn't seem to share Rosie's concerns.

"How come you didn't tell your ideas in class yesterday?" Wolfie asked. "I told lots of mine."

"I remember," Rosie said.

"We have to tell Mrs Marshall our four parts today, you know," Wolfie said.

"I know," Rosie said.

"I have about a million ideas. I can't even decide which one to write about," Wolfie said. "Do you want to use one of mine?"

"No, thanks. I have my own."

"I know who my hero is going to be. Have you got yours yet, Rosie?"

Rosie shrugged. "Maybe." She wasn't ready to talk about it yet.

"Mrs Marshall said we can use people we know as inspiration." He smiled extra big at her.

"I *know*, Wolfie," Rosie said.

"Just sayin', I can think of a good hero, if you need someone," Wolfie said. He stood up from his seat, put his fists on his hips and puffed his chest out.

The bus's brakes squealed, and Wolfie lost his balance. "Sit down!" yelled the driver.

Rosie put her hand over her mouth to hide her giggle as Wolfie sat down. *That Wolfie.* A story about him would be more ridiculous than one about oat milkmaids.

Or would it?

What if Gram was right? What if a bad idea really *could* turn into a good idea?

Wolfie scrunched his face. "What?" he said. "Why did your eyes just go so big?"

Rosie pointed at Wolfie. "You just gave me an idea."

Now Wolfie's eyes went big too. "Whoa. You're going to make me your hero, aren't you? I *knew* it! What's the problem I get to solve?"

The bus pulled to a stop.

"We're here," Rosie said, sliding her arms into her backpack.

"C'mon, Rosie! How am I going to save the day?"

Rosie's eyebrows double jumped. "We'll see," she said, and walked to the front of the bus.

Chapter Seven

A silent conversation

Mrs Marshall told the class that tonight's homework would be to write a rough draft of their story. That meant you told your story using all four parts, but it was just a first try. The next day, they would do revisions, which meant changing some things to make the story even better. But today, they had to share their story plans with Mrs Marshall.

Wolfie was called up to the teacher's desk first. While he was gone, Rosie quickly pulled out her trusty red notebook and wrote down the idea she'd had on the bus. Then she closed her notebook.

When Wolfie came back, he told Rosie that Mrs Marshall had helped him decide which idea to write about. "And I'm going to start right now!" he said. "I might even have time to write *two* stories if I go fast enough."

Rosie didn't know whether writing fast was a good thing.

When it was Rosie's turn, she showed her notebook to Mrs Marshall.

EVERY STORY NEEDS:

SETTING: where the story happens FOREST

HERO: most important character MOUSE?

PROBLEM: something wrong that the
        hero has to fix or solve WOLF?

SOLUTION: how they fix it

Mrs Marshall nodded as she read
through Rosie's story plan. She put a
turquoise-painted fingertip on *WOLF?*
and looked up at Rosie. Then her eyes
moved over to Wolfie while her eyebrows
rose in a question. Rosie shrugged, and
she felt her cheeks getting warm as she
smiled. Mrs Marshall smiled too and

gave Rosie a little wink. It was like they had a whole conversation without saying a word.

"Well, Rosie, you have a good start here. Seems like the only thing you're missing is a solution." She pointed at the ice-cream cone. "Maybe this has something to do with it?"

"Maybe," Rosie said, and smiled.

When Rosie went back to her table, she put her trusty red notebook at the bottom of her book pile. She didn't want Wolfie to see her notes. He still thought he was going to be the hero in her story. She didn't know how to tell him that he had actually given her an idea for the *problem*.

It was a good idea too. She just wasn't sure Wolfie would agree.

Chapter Eight

Run away

When they got off the bus that afternoon, Wolfie asked Rosie if she wanted to meet up at the playground later. Wednesdays were Gram's day to work late at the library, so Rosie usually went to the park. But not today. She had a whole rough draft to write, and she hadn't even decided on a solution yet.

"Sorry," she said. "I'm going to be busy."

"Doing what?" asked Wolfie.

Rosie just stared at him. Was he kidding?

"Oh, your story?" Wolfie said. "Okay. I've already finished mine. Maybe I'll write another one tonight and decide which one I like better."

"Okay, Wolfie." Rosie tried not to sound annoyed. Why was this so easy for Wolfie and so hard for her? Suddenly, Rosie couldn't wait to get home.

"I'll see you tomorrow," she mumbled, and she started to run.

"Hey, Rosie, wait!" Wolfie called. He sprinted after her, but Rosie had the wind under her feet. As she turned up her drive, she glanced back down the street to see Wolfie doubled over and panting in front of his house.

Rosie said hi to Dad and got herself a snack: biscuits from the cupboard, made with actual sugar. Rosie loved going to Gram's, but Dad always had tastier snacks.

Rosie wiped the sweat off her forehead as she flopped onto her bed and kicked her smelly trainers to the other side of the room. She peeled off her soggy socks and wiggled her toes in the cool air. Then she opened her trusty red notebook and read over her story plan. Just one thing was missing, and she filled it in:

SOLUTION: how they fix it RUN AWAY

Rosie lay back on her bed and stared up at the ceiling. She imagined a forest of trees filling the blank space. She heard the rustling of the leaves, the hooting of an owl. She smelled the sweet, fresh scent of the fir trees.

She saw a little grey mouse scamper through the pine needles on the forest floor. Behind the mouse crept a big, brown wolf, drooling as it silently followed its prey. Rosie gave a little shiver as the mouse looked over her shoulder, caught a glimpse of the wolf and started to run for her life.

Rosie flipped a page over, turning to a clean page in her notebook, and wrote:

Once upon a time . . .

By the time Dad had called her down for dinner, Rosie had finished her rough draft. It was a whole story, with all the parts Mrs Marshall said they needed. It was okay, Rosie thought, but it was still missing the secret ingredient. She needed a twist.

Chapter Nine

Heroic features

By Thursday morning, Rosie had already had some ideas for revisions. But with Wolfie sitting right there at her table, she didn't dare open her notebook.

Mrs Marshall called her over for a discussion. "You've got all four parts here, Rosie. How are you feeling about your story?"

Rosie sighed. "I don't think it's right yet."

Mrs Marshall nodded. "That's what revisions are for. What would you like to change?"

Rosie shuffled her feet. She still hadn't told Mrs Marshall about her secret ingredient. What if she couldn't come up with a twist? "I don't know," Rosie mumbled.

"It will come to you," Mrs Marshall assured her.

But Rosie was feeling doubtful.

After school, Rosie headed for Gram's to work on revisions and make her final draft. She hoped Gram's brain food might help her think of a clever twist. She was passing through the playground when Wolfie came jogging up to her.

"Hey, Rosie, do you want to interview me?"

Rosie laughed, but Wolfie was waiting for an answer. "What for?" she asked.

"So you can add more details when

you revise your hero. Duh." Wolfie
smiled his toothy grin.

"Oh, um . . . thanks, but I think I've
got everything I need."

"Have it your way," said Wolfie with a
shrug. "But you'd better take a good look
at me so you can describe all my heroic
features." He climbed up on a big rock
and held his arms in a muscle pose.

Rosie laughed again. "Heroic features?" She tilted her head to the side. "Like what?"

Wolfie jumped down. He stuck his face right into Rosie's and stared at her. "Big eyes, good for seeing bad guys coming."

"Ohhh-kaaay," said Rosie.

"Big ears, good for hearing dangerous beasts." Wolfie set his feet wide, put his hands on his sides and turned his head back and forth like an owl.

"Uh-huh," said Rosie.

"A big ol' nose, good at sniffing out solutions." Wolfie leaned in close to Rosie and inhaled loudly.

"Ew." Rosie put her hands up in front of her and took a step back.

"And just look at this priceless smile." Wolfie bared all his teeth in a ridiculous grin. "I'd win any hero contest no problem, right?"

Rosie's mouth popped open. "Contest?" An idea was twisting its way into her brain.

"Well?" Wolfie said. "Wouldn't I? Huh, Rosie?"

Rosie patted Wolfie on the shoulder, pumping her eyebrows. "You're a winner, alright." She started running down the path towards Gram's. "I've gotta go, Wolfie!" she called over her shoulder. "See you tomorrow!"

"Yeah, see ya!" he called back. "We're gonna read our stories to the whole class!"

"I *know*!" Rosie shook her head as she broke into a run. *That Wolfie.*

"How's the story coming?" Gram asked

when Rosie popped through the door.

"I think I've just worked out my secret ingredient!" she said breathlessly.

"Well then, I guess you'd better take a grain-free carrot-fig bar and get to work!"

Rosie piled a plate with brain food and took it to her nook. She pulled out her trusty red notebook and made a few changes to her notes.

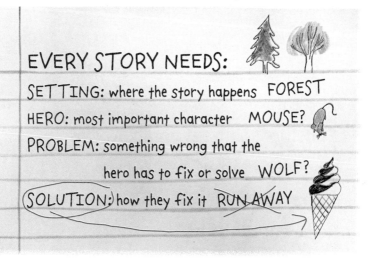

EVERY STORY NEEDS:

SETTING: where the story happens   FOREST

HERO: most important character   MOUSE?

PROBLEM: something wrong that the
        hero has to fix or solve   WOLF?

SOLUTION: how they fix it   RUN AWAY

Then she started revising her story. She crossed out lines and wrote new ones. She erased and added and moved things around. She didn't look up from her notebook until she had finished. Then she took a deep breath, stretched and ate her brain food while she read through the whole thing.

Feeling satisfied, she copied her story onto a clean page – without carrot-fig crumbs. Then she added some pictures on the sides. She read it over again and smiled.

This is a pretty good story! she thought.

Before she went home, Rosie practised reading her story aloud to Gram. Gram let out a big laugh when Rosie got to the end.

"You like it?" Rosie asked.

"I love it! You remembered what I told you," Gram said.

"Clever is better than strong?"

Gram pressed her finger on Rosie's nose. "You got it, my little red Rose."

Rosie was excited about her story, but as she got ready for bed that night, a worry crept in. How would Wolfie feel about it? He had been so sure Rosie would use him as her hero. And she *had* used Wolfie for inspiration, but . . .

What if he didn't like the way she'd put him in the story?

What if he thought she'd tricked him?

What if she hurt his feelings?

Now it felt like there really was a storm in her brain. Rosie had a hard time falling asleep.

Chapter Ten

Story time

At the bus stop in the morning, Wolfie told Rosie *all* about his story. He kept talking the whole way to school.

OK, so the villain is this evil genius SPY, and the hero is this boy who is just trying to go to school, but he ACTUALLY has a secret code that got programmed into his BRAIN and he didn't even know about it . . .

Rosie tried to listen, but she was getting more and more anxious. She was sure her story was good. But she was still worried about what Wolfie would think.

Wolfie volunteered to read first. His story was very long, and it really was exciting. In fact, Rosie got so interested in Wolfie's story that she forgot to be worried for a few minutes. When Wolfie finished, he took a bow. Rosie smiled at him and gave a double thumbs-up.

But while other kids were reading their stories, Rosie felt worry spreading through her whole body. By the time her turn came, she could feel her heart beating all the way down to her little toes. Rosie stood up and took a deep breath. Then she started to read.

THE MOUSE AND THE WOLF

by Rosie Woods

Once upon a time, by a rocky stream in the forest, a mouse was looking for food. She found some hunters sitting on rocks, eating their lunch. She sneaked around their feet. She nibbled on their crumbs. She filled up her cheeks with more crumbs to take home for her babies.

While she was eating, she listened to the hunters. They were talking about what they would do if they saw a wolf. They were humans. They had all kinds of plans for wolves. The only plan the mouse had if she saw a wolf was to run away.

Unfortunately, on her way home, the mouse was so excited about her crumbs that she didn't see the wolf coming. Instead of running away, she ran straight into him!

The wolf picked the mouse up by the tail. He dangled her right in front of his terrifying face. "Hello, lunch," he said.

The mouse looked into his evil yellow eyes. "Oh, hello," she said. All the crumbs tumbled out of her mouth. What could she say so the wolf wouldn't eat her? She thought fast.

"What big, golden eyes you have," said the mouse.

"Thanks," said the wolf. "I get them from my mum."

A long string of wolf snot was hanging from the wolf's nose. The mouse almost hit it every time she swung closer to him.

"Your nose is so ... shiny," said the mouse.

"I can smell a rodent a mile away," the wolf said proudly.

The mouse's new plan seemed to be working.

"What big, fluffy ears you have," said the mouse.

"I can hear an ant crawling across a leaf." The wolf grinned.

"And look at that perfect smile!" said the mouse. "Wow, you know what? You just might win ..."

"Win what?" said the wolf.

"The World's Wonderfulest Wolf Contest!" said the mouse.

"What? Where? When?" asked the wolf. He seemed pretty excited.

"The humans are having it over by the rocky stream," said the mouse. "If you hurry, they might still let you enter."

The wolf dropped the mouse and raced to the rocky stream. And the mouse gathered up her crumbs and raced for home. THE END

Chapter Eleven

No problem

After Rosie finished reading her story, it was breaktime. Wolfie came up to her on the playground. She held her breath and waited for him to ask why she hadn't made him the hero of her story.

"Hey, Rosie! You really did put me in your story! Wolfie? Wolf? That's me, right?"

Rosie bit her lip and nodded.

"And those hunters – they were going to get the wolf, weren't they?"

Rosie scuffed her foot and examined the little cloud of dust it stirred up.

"Mm-hmm."

"Ha! That's awesome! That mouse was so clever," Wolfie said.

Rosie's head popped up. "You're not angry?"

"Angry?" Wolfie looked confused. "Why would I be angry?"

"Well . . ." Rosie shrugged. "Because the wolf wasn't the hero?"

Wolfie laughed. "Who cares? Every story needs a villain." Wolfie held his hands up like claws and growled.

"You mean it?"

"Yeah! It's fun to be the bad guy." Wolfie punched the air. "Pow! Boom! Gotcha!"

Rosie laughed. *That Wolfie.* "Pow!" she said, and air-punched back at Wolfie. He was right – it was kind of fun.

"Hey," she said, "thanks for giving me the idea."

"No problem. I'm full of great ideas," Wolfie said.

"Yeah," Rosie said. She had to admit this was true. "I couldn't have done it without you."

"Of course you could. You know why?" Wolfie asked.

"Why?"

"Because you're a great writer!"

And for once, Rosie didn't mind Wolfie telling her something she already knew.

Discussion questions

1. In this book, what is the **setting**? What are some of the different places that Rosie goes to throughout the book?

2. Who is the **hero** of this story? Can you name three other important characters?

3. What is the **problem** Rosie has to solve? Why is it important for her to solve it?

4. Who gave Rosie an idea for the **solution** to her problem?

5. Rosie likes a story with a clever **twist** – when something doesn't go the way you're expecting. What was the twist in Rosie's story about the mouse and the wolf? What was the twist in this book?

6. Find the story "Little Red Riding Hood" in your library or online. How many things can you find in this book that remind you of the original story?

Digging Deeper

Who can write a good story? Anyone! In this book, Rosie and Wolfie were writing fiction, or stories from their imaginations. But whether you're making up a story or writing about something real (non-fiction), think about answering six questions: WHO? WHAT? WHEN? WHERE? WHY? and HOW?

BRAINSTORM When you brainstorm, you write down *all* your ideas. You never know when a bad idea might turn into a good one! You can brainstorm answers to all six questions. There are no right or wrong answers.

SETTING The setting of your story answers the questions WHERE? and WHEN? Does your story happen inside or outside? In another room or on another planet? Did your story happen a long time ago, will it happen in the future, or is it happening right now?

HERO The hero is the main character: the most important WHO? of your story. You'll have other characters, too — some good, some bad — but your hero is the one who will work out how to solve the main problem. What does your hero look like? What kind of personality do they have? What is their favourite thing to do? Least favourite thing?

PROBLEM This is the WHAT? part: what are the characters doing, what's going on around them – and what's wrong with the situation? Something must be wrong, because for a story to be interesting, something needs to change. So part of the WHAT? is the WHY?: why does it need to change?

SOLUTION The solution is the HOW? part of the story: how does your hero fix what's wrong? And how did they work out what they needed to do? Don't make it too easy for them! If it was hard work for the hero to work out the solution, then it's even more satisfying when they get it right.

ROUGH DRAFT Once you've worked out the answers to all these questions, you can write a rough draft. Write about WHO is doing something, WHERE and WHEN it's happening, WHAT's going on and WHY something needs to change, and HOW the hero changes it. Now you have a story – but wait! It's probably not finished yet.

REVISION Revision means changing your story to make it better. You might change words, characters, descriptions or actions. You might change the order of when things happen. When you think you've finished, try reading your story aloud to yourself or to a friend. You may think of even more ways to improve this story before you've finally finished.

About the author

photo by Robert Webb

Maya Myers writes books for children and edits books for children and adults. She's a former teacher and loves cooking, gardening and (of course) reading – just like Rosie! Originally from Maine, USA, Maya now lives in North Carolina, where she grows lots of vegetables, including beans, in her garden. She has three children, six chickens and a large cat called Hoss.

About the illustrator

photo by Jayden Campbell Photography

Eleanor Howell is a British writer and illustrator living in Toronto, Canada. She is interested in storytelling in its many forms, and has two master's degrees in Museum Studies and Archiving and is embarking on her third degree, in English Literature. Eleanor loves reading, walking and eating chocolate, but has yet to master the art of doing all three at the same time.